Why I Love
School

Illustrated by Daniel Howarth

HarperCollins *Children's Books*

I love school because...

I have a special backpack.

I love school because...

my teacher is nice.

I love school because...

at lunchtime we play together.

I love school because...

we make cool things.

I love school because...
I can spend the day with my friends.

I love school because...

we have lunch together.

I love school because...
we go on school trips.

we put on a school play.

I love school because...

we get to come back tomorrow!

Everyone loves school,

especially... ME!

First published in hardback in Great Britain by HarperCollins Children's Books in 2017
This edition published in 2019

3 5 7 9 10 8 6 4 2

978-0-00-797702-4

HarperCollins Children's Books is a division of HarperCollins Publishers Ltd.

Text and illustrations copyright © HarperCollins Publishers Ltd 2017

A CIP catalogue record for this title is available from the British Library.
Visit our website at www.harpercollins.co.uk

Printed in China